# THURGOOD MARSHALL

## DISCOVER THE LIFE OF AN AMERICAN LEGEND

Don McLeese

Rourke

**Publishing LLC**

Vero Beach, Florida 32964

www.rourkepublishing.com

PHOTO CREDITS: All photos Library of Congress

Cover: *Thurgood Marshall as a younger man*

Editor: Frank Sloan

Cover design by Nicola Stratford

**Library of Congress Cataloging-in-Publication Data**

McLeese, Don.
  Thurgood Marshall / Don McLeese.
    p. cm. — (Discover the life of an American legend)
Includes bibliographical references and index.
  ISBN 1-58952-303-2 (hardcover)
  1. Marshall, Thurgood, 1908-1993—Juvenile literature. 2.
Afro-American judges—United States—Biography--Juvenile literature. [1.
Marshall, Thurgood, 1908-1993. 2. Lawyers. 3. Judges. 4. United States.
Supreme Court—Biography. 5. African Americans—Biography.] I.
Marshall, Thurgood, 1908-1993. II. Title. III. American legends (Vero
Beach, Fla.)
  KF8745.M34 M38 2002
  347.73'2634—dc21

                                              2002004152

Printed in the USA

w/w

# TABLE OF CONTENTS

# "MR. CIVIL RIGHTS"

Thurgood Marshall was the first **African American** to become a **justice** of the **Supreme Court**. He was named by President Lyndon Johnson to the highest court in the country in 1967. Before that, Thurgood had been a great **lawyer**. He won many Supreme Court cases that protected the **civil rights** of African Americans. He was known as "Mr. Civil Rights."

*Thurgood in front of the*
*Supreme Court building, 1958*

# GRANDSON OF A SLAVE

Thurgood was born in Baltimore, Maryland, on July 2, 1908. His father, William, was a waiter on a railroad dining car. Later he worked at an all-white club. His mother, Norma, was a teacher. Thurgood was named after his grandfather, Thoroughgood. He had been a **slave** and then a soldier during the **Civil War**.

*A slave's grandson became one of the country's most powerful African Americans.*

# GREAT STUDENT

Both of his parents believed in a good education. Thurgood made them proud because he was so smart in school. In those days, African Americans usually went to different schools than white students. The law said schools could be "separate but equal." Thurgood knew that if the schools were separate, they weren't really equal.

# COLLEGE PROTEST

In 1925, Thurgood went to college at Lincoln University in Pennsylvania. One night, he and friends went to a movie theater. They sat on the main floor, where whites did, even after an usher asked them to move to the balcony. "I guess that's what started the whole thing," Thurgood said of his first civil-rights protest.

*Thurgood at a civil rights meeting*

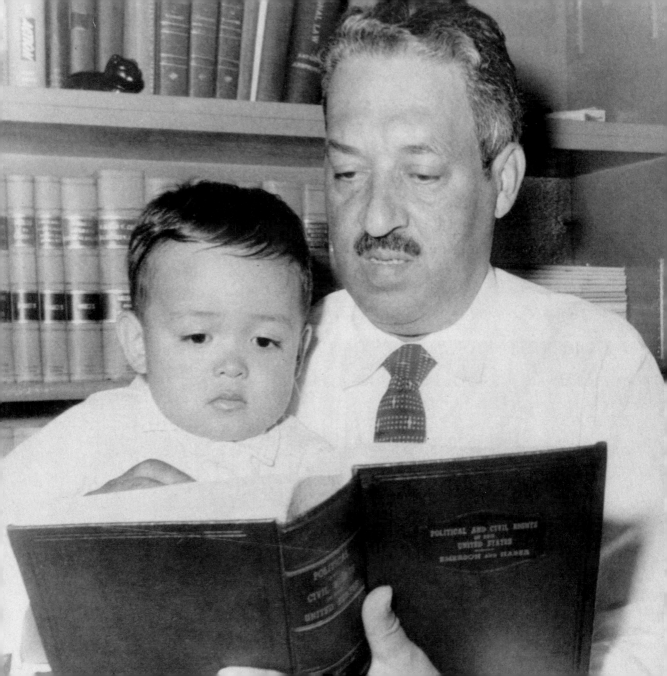

# "WHITES ONLY"

After graduating from college, Thurgood wanted to be a lawyer. He applied to the University of Maryland Law School, but the school turned him down. His grades were good enough, but the school had never accepted an African American student. Instead, Thurgood went to Howard University in Washington, D.C.

*Thurgood in his law library with his son*

# CIVIL RIGHTS LAW

At Howard, Thurgood realized that a lawyer could help change laws that were unfair to African Americans. He wanted to help African Americans enjoy the same civil rights as any other American. He graduated with honors in 1933. Then he went home to Baltimore and opened his law office. He didn't charge people who were too poor to pay.

*Thurgood wanted to change unfair laws.*

# A BIG CASE

In 1935, another African American student tried to get into the University of Maryland Law School. When he was turned down, he went to court with Thurgood to change the school's unfair rules. A Maryland **judge** agreed that the state's law school should not judge on the basis of color. Thurgood had won his first big case.

*Thurgood leaving a federal courthouse*

# FAMOUS LAWYER

Thurgood became one of the most famous lawyers in the country. He took 32 cases to the Supreme Court and won 29 of them! The biggest was in 1954. This happened when Brown v. Board of Education of Topeka ended the "separate but equal" policy. The court said that African American students must be allowed to attend the same schools as whites.

*Thurgood sitting beneath a portrait of Justice Louis Brandeis*

# SUPREME JUSTICE

In 1961, Thurgood Marshall became a judge. He was as great a judge as he had been as a lawyer. Only the best judges are named to the Supreme Court, which Thurgood joined in 1967.

*The Supreme Court building in Washington, D.C.*

Thurgood Marshall was the Supreme Court's first African American. He retired from the court in 1991. He died on January 24, 1993.

# GLOSSARY

**African American** (aff RIH kun uh MARE ih kun) — a black person, an American whose early relatives came from Africa.

**civil rights** (SIV ul RYTS) — the equal rights of every citizen in the country.

**civil war** ( SIV ul WAHR) — war in the United States between the North and the South, 1861-1865

**judge** (JUHJ) — in a court of law, the person who decides on disagreements and determines innocence or guilt.

**justice** (JUH stiss) — a judge of the Supreme Court.

**lawyer** (LAW yuhr) — a person who advises about legal rights.

**slave** (SLAYV) — someone who is owned by another person and works for no money

**Supreme Court** (suh PREEM CORT) — the highest court in the United States.

# INDEX

## Further Reading

Gibson, Karen Bush. *Thurgood Marshall: A Photo-Illustrated Biography.* Capstone
   Press, 2002.
Williams, Carla. *Thurgood Marshall.* Child's World Incorporated, 2002.

## Websites To Visit

http://www.ai.mit.edu/~isbell/HFh/black/events_and_people/html/001.thurgood_mar
   shall.html
http://library.thinkquest.org/3337/tmarsh.html

## About The Author

Don McLeese is an award-winning journalist whose work has appeared in many
newspapers and magazines. He is a frequent contributor to the World Book
Encyclopedia. He and his wife, Maria, have two daughters and live in West Des
Moines, Iowa.